Published by

Goffaramma Press

Www.TheSuccessfulZombie.com

Copywrite 2020

ISBN 9781671567160

The Successful Zombie

Prologue

"I'm writing all of this down, what I know to be true, because I felt the fear in a dream and it rides inside my head like an anchored ship. There's no way to prevent it. The only way to confront the inevitable is to prepare." ~ Randy Quaid; Actor, Survivalist.

It will soon be upon us, and it won't be what you think. The real world account will be flipped, opposing what you'd expect from the showbiz versions you're used to watching on a screen and reading about in books or graphic novels. The difference in what you've been fed by pop-culture and television shows is that instead of the story being about the surviving humans fighting each day to stay alive, the real story is that the dead will outnumber the living 10,000 to 1. Our story, the true and eventual story, is that we won't know what it's like to be a human after the Zombie Apocalypse unfolds. What we will experience, once it is upon us, is a sleepwalking nightmare.

We'd all like to think that we're going to be one of the 'lucky' few human survivors, but in reality, most of us will be among the walking dead. There is truth in what we've read and seen regarding the ensuing Zombie Apocalypse. The movies, the books, and all the online reference material suggests that 99.99% of the population, however it occurs, will become zombies. Those who remain human will amount to less than 0.01% of the entire populace. You will not survive the Zombie Apocalypse as a human. The most likely outcome for you and everyone you know is that you will all become zombies. This is fact. The images in your head of what will come should haunt you. Bargain for your lucidity in each and every breath, hoping for death before the Apocalypse ensues. Your suffering is significant only for your awareness of what will be upon us soon enough. It will happen, and when it does, you need to be ready.

Part of the preparation includes maintaining a bit of levity. My purpose is to prepare us, but with facts and statistics that have been vetted by those who have higher degrees and better insight than I.

It's true, we'll be eating the brains of the few human survivors left on Earth, but we can prepare to do so with the absurdity of the situation in mind. For instance, becoming a zombie is scary, but one upside could be that we won't be running from zombies trying to stay alive. We'll be dead. Again, I don't want to be a zombie, however it really might not be that bad. This is our truth, and life is just another step in our evolution towards whatever comes next, and what comes next for us is becoming zombies.

And the fact is, once we're all zombies, we'll all be competing for the precious few human brains that will be left on Earth. We'll all be craving brains, and it seems that brains will be in very short supply. For those unbelievers who refuse to accept what it means to be a zombie, listen up. You can't escape what will happen. It has already been decided, and you will most assuredly have a hankering for brains. Consuming brains will be the only motivator to your existence. Nothing else will matter. You will be an unstoppable force willing to chase down what is left of the mortal populace. You won't know what it means to quit, and you will not give up.

This existence is the destiny of almost the entirety of the Earth's human population, and that includes you. Whether you're an athlete or a couch potato, an old grandma or a little baby. When you become a zombie, you'll be a brain-hungry whatever-you-are, and you'll be searching for food.

This book is a vital how-to guide for everyone living today. As the Zombie Apocalypse approaches, preparation is paramount. By the time you are a zombie, you won't be able to read much less comprehend the tactics and measures it will take to be a successful zombie. Take your time reading this book and commit anything you can to the deepest recesses of your memory. As a zombie, you will only remember the most basic human functions, but you will also have vague memories of being human. Make it your mission to remember the facts of this book. If you can do this, you will have a better chance of surviving the Zombie Apocalypse as a successful zombie.

This book also explains the uses of your survival kit fanny pack. As a zombie, you'll need some basic supplies.

It has been decided that the best way to house these supplies and keep them with you at all times is by wearing a fanny pack. As a human with a rudimentary understanding of fashion, you would not be caught dead wearing a fanny pack. Once a zombie, being caught dead wearing a fanny pack will be the name of the game. You will be dead, and successful zombies will be wearing fanny packs with essential supplies. This book is not meant to offend those who enjoy fanny packs as living humans. If you are one of those people who happen to own and wear a fanny pack (old people, foreigners, etc.) just look at it this way, you're ahead of the game when we all turn to zombies. For those of us who don't have the fanny pack yet, get one, and fill it with gum, dental floss, and a whistle. All of these essentials will be explained along with how, as a zombie, you will use them, later in the book.

Now let's get started. Preparing for the Zombie Apocalypse cannot be done too soon. The sooner you read this book, prepare yourself, and feel comfortable with your impending change into the zombie state, the sooner you'll be prepared for that eventuality. Don't be a quitter.

Anything worth doing is worth doing right, and as Lee Iacocca put it so eloquently, "The thing that lies at the foundation of positive change, the way I see it, is service to a fellow human being." I see it that way too, and this book is dedicated to that idea. My goal is to be of service to you, the reader, to prepare you for leadership in our post apocalyptic world of zombies eating brains out of the remaining humans.

Chapter 1

Eating Brains

First thing's first. You're going to have to eat brains. That's a given. Not an appetizing thought to you now, but by the time you've turned into a zombie, it'll be akin to eating a hamburger or pizza on an empty stomach. To eat brains, you'll have to catch humans. To catch humans, you're going to have to be clever. It won't be easy, because if we've learned anything from the movies, zombies are slow, dumb, and easily fooled. What you will have going for you is that you won't have to sleep, and you'll be determined.

You'll be competing with other zombies, but they'll all be as dumb as you will be. All zombies function on a level playing field. They roam in packs, but no zombie is smarter than another. You can use this to your advantage, but the best way to capture a human will be to hide and wait for them to either sleep, or go to the bathroom. When they're sleeping, they're obviously an easy target. You might even get a good bite or two in before they wake up, and by that time, too late tasty human. The human is dead, and you're feasting on a big juicy brain. One useful tactic, if you can manage it, is the ability to lie in wait for a human to happen upon you. This takes skill and stamina, and although you will be a slow, dimwitted zombie, it will be more difficult than you can imagine. The main reason waiting for long periods of time is tough for zombies, is that zombies quickly forget what they are doing and why. You may decide to hide in a particular place, but after a short time, you will wonder what you're doing and most likely move along. This is a foreseeable difficult task for a run-of-the-mill zombie, so you must practice this maneuver in order to perfect it as a human. If perfected in your living state, once you're among the walking dead, you'll have it down pat. Schedule some time to sit in an area of your house or garden for a period of time doing nothing. Do not read a book or entertain yourself with thought. Sit and do nothing. Don't even close your eyes. This may cause slumber, and the next thing you know you'll be waking up from a nap in the yard having wasted your time unconscious. Stay awake. Keep your eyes open, but your brain on pause. When you can perfect this scenario, you should be able to transfer your new skill to your eventual zombie state.

I use this as an example because you must be aware that right now, you're studying for a test sober, which you will effectively be taking at a later date, drunk out of your mind. Aim for perfection, and you might just get lucky.

Chapter 2

Preparation 101

We all need to accept our days as humans are numbered. My sincere desire is to manage the completion of this book in order to be read and remembered by you, the reader, before the poop hits the fan. I assume I'll finish this book before the Zombie Apocalypse, but I could just be wasting my time. If you're reading this though, I've made my deadline. Thank the good lord above.

So these are your last days as a human. You might have only a few days left, or if we're lucky, the Zombie Apocalypse won't happen for many years. The time table I do not know, but I do believe it will be by design rather than by happenstance. That's right, the entire thing could be orchestrated by an unknown group who have that power to begin this world's nightmare. I cannot say who they are, but it really could be anyone, from Elon Musk to the Taco Bell executives. Regardless, you need to be preparing as a human to be the best zombie you can be. All of the ideas I suggest are based in factual knowledge that I alone understand. Your acceptance will save you. Your denial will result in the horrors of an unsuccessful play to remain among the dimwitted semi-conscious swine. You will expire, aborted by your idiot peers into the dirt. So it's up to you, but I'd take seriously the words I have prepared for you within this book.

Let's start with the basics. First, you must identify all the redheads you commonly see out in public. Red headed people, it is assumed, are the most resilient to any zombie-fication of the human species. After considerable research, I have found that zombies as depicted in Hollywood movies are rarely red headed. In fact, there are heroes within the Hollywood zombie movies that are indeed red headed themselves. Why look at zombie movies and their casting to predict types of zombie immunities? The fact is there are factions of Hollywood who may have their hand in the eventual outbreak that leads to the Zombie Apocalypse. As I stated before, we don't know who will start this thing, but I have been made privy to certain information that has compelled me to write this how-to guide with the intent to prepare the general public for what is inevitable. I can't divulge certain information about my sources, but I can say that what

I am writing is based in factual information. Therefore, when I present information, such as the Hollywood connection to predicting future events, please take it seriously.

With the red head information in mind, identify all those unlucky red heads you'll be eating brains out of later, and make note of where you see them and where they live, if possible. As a caveat however, don't go stalking red heads. We still live in a society, and stalking is a crime. Red headed people are not targets of any kind right now, as long as you are human. Just make note of where they are. In fact, you most likely have a friend or two with red hair. Just keep them in mind as a brain oven for your future consumption as a zombie. Red hair is a beautiful thing, and by no means am I suggesting you or anyone else should cause any harm to a red headed person. This is not the direction I'm going with this. I'm just trying to help your future zombie self when you're looking for brains. That is all. So again, no harm to the red heads. Just keep them on your radar.

By the way, if you are a red head yourself, don't assume you'll remain human as the Zombie Apocalypse rains down upon us. The *red head is immune* idea is just a theory. If I was you, and I was identified as a Ginger, as they say, I'd keep reading. If for no other reason than to be prepared for the smart zombies this book will most definitely produce.

Chapter 3

Likely Areas of Human Survivors

So if we can assume from my extensive research that the Zombie Apocalypse is coming, and we can agree that most of us will become zombies when the aforementioned Zombie Apocalypse begins, we can also arrive at the conclusion that those in remote areas of the world with little to no access to society will remain human longer than most. For instance, if a cruise ship is out at sea when the outbreak occurs, those humans will most likely be uncontaminated. Therefore, when they arrive into port, they'll essentially be fish in a barrel for the rest of us who will be zombies, looking for fresh brains.

Let's take this a step further. Remote villages, populated islands, or possibly even the entire country of Australia, could be sequestered enough to remain entirely human. Given that international flights happen by the thousands each day, we may not see many areas of uncontaminated humans, but for argument's sake, we need to take every possibility into consideration. So wherever they may be, these places will lure zombies to them, and the zombies who are closest to these areas will be the first to get there, obviously. To become a successful zombie from the start, you need to research these secluded types of areas that are closest to your present geographical location. These areas will be your first stops as a successful zombie. Depending on where you live, you may find that a sea port is your best bet, or possibly a secluded cabin village. It all depends on where you live. Whatever the case may be, figure it out now, make a note of it, and memorize how to get there. Once again, as a zombie, you'll be lucky to remember the most basic of facts, so commit yourself to memorizing your most likely food sources. And it should go without saying, you'll need to be able to walk there. As a zombie, you will lack the coordination and agility to drive a car. Once a zombie, you may get a car started as that will be a muscle memory type of function once you're the walking dead. Starting a car is a basic maneuver most of us will remember as zombies. Taking a leisurely drive out on the road to pick up some bread and brains will not be happening, however. A zombie driving a car never ends well, so let that dream die with you. You're walking.

The secluded and/or completely separate areas that you designate as being within zombie-walking-distance can also be noted on a map of some sort. If you can design a simple diagram noting the general direction you'll need to go in order to get there once you're a zombie, it could very well be of use to your future zombie self. I can't say if it'll be a foolproof method of brain discovery for you, but it's worth a shot. Hey man, you need all the help you can get. Do what you can to improve your odds.

So to sum up this chapter, identifying where secluded humans might be is a step you must take now. Figure it out, write it down, memorize it, and make sure you can walk there.

Chapter 4

What Exactly is a Successful Zombie?

You might be wondering what I mean by "successful" when it comes to being a zombie. You're thinking clearly and asking the right questions if so. I commend you.

A successful zombie will be one who can keep their wits about them, find remaining humans, be able to capture said humans to eat their brains, and most importantly, lead a pack of zombies to do the dirty work for them. Success as a zombie is similar in nature to success as a human. Many successful humans are leaders. They understand other humans and can be "The Boss". A successful zombie will need to be a "boss" as well. This won't be easy as I've made mention in previous chapters, zombies are slow and dumb. They don't follow each other, but rather just wonder around in packs, assumingly because none of them really know what's going on. That's where you, the successful zombie, will use your skills to achieve what other zombies can't. What you must do is practice your skills as a leader now, as a human. Coach a little league team. Start a club or organization to help others. Become a Boy Scout leader. Do something where you can practice and perfect your leadership skills. Get to know your team and be a positive role model. Allow them to trust you by making good decisions and listening to their concerns. Earn their trust, and then make good decisions on their behalf.

Now, here's the important part. This is where you parlay your honest and trustworthy leadership skills into a solid leader of the walking dead. Those you lead as a human will become the zombies you will lead as a zombie. Let me repeat that. Whomever you lead now, as a human, will be the zombies you will lead after the Zombie Apocalypse begins. Their basic human memories will remain intact, and once zombies, they'll assume you are still their leader. You see, you're training them now to be your zombie lackeys. Today they're Boy Scout troupe 395, tomorrow (after the Zombie Apocalypse) they're your zombie horde catching and delivering human brains to your doorstep. It's the perfect set-up! Plan today for what you need tomorrow. This is what makes a successful zombie.

So let me expand on that thought for a moment. I'll let you in on a little secret. Right now, I am the coach for my son's little league team. I'm also the room parent for my daughter's fourth grade class. In addition, I run a fantasy football league and I'm a leader in my community, organizing fun runs and mud runs. I also began a model train group at the local high school of which there are now over fifty members. And to top it all off, I've chosen teaching as my profession and I teach over 140 students as a middle school math teacher. Do you think I do this because I'm a natural leader and love getting out and being a social butterfly!? Hell no! I'm preparing my friend! I'm leading all these young folks and community members so I can later be their zombie leader. That, my man, is why I do what I do.

Chapter 5

Zombie Food Quotas

As a zombie, your survival depends on eating human brains. The problem lies in the amount of human brains that will be available. With 0.01% of the population remaining human once the Zombie Apocalypse goes into effect, there won't be many brains to sustain the enormous number of zombies roaming the planet. Luckily, you made the wise choice of purchasing this book, so you will be prepared to combat the human brain shortage that most certainly will affect the zombie population.

As I stated before, you must become a leader of zombies. Honing your skills and becoming a human leader of some sort in the present zombie-less world we live in now will serve you well in our future zombie world, in more ways than one. If you can become a successful zombie leader, you will already possess the skills it will take to sustain a human brain-rich environment. As a leader, you will need to create and sustain a sizable, well programmed "camp" of humans. You will need many humans, and you will need to protect and nurture your human farm in order for it to produce an everlasting supply of human brains. The most efficient and productive way of doing this is to be a solid and trustworthy zombie leader who can configure, maintain, and manage a community of humans.

Configuring your human brain farm will take extensive planning as a human so that when you become a zombie, you will remember and understand its value. The reasoning behind your farm relates to the demand for human brains. Simply put, if you don't plan in advance, you will eventually run out of food, effectively ridding the planet of not only humans, but the populace of the evolutionary inheritors of the Earth, you and your fellow zombies. The planet will be left to the insects and plants, hurdling through space with only relics of its once beautiful menagerie of living organisms. We cannot let this happen. As a successful zombie, you will sustain yourself by allowing humans to continue to procreate and live in a controlled society, managed by you and your zombie followers.

So how does this work? It works by supplying humans with all of their basic needs, permitting them to live within a community and allowing them to feel safe. If you manage this correctly, they will thrive, procreating and sustaining a population of healthy humans, supplying your zombie brothers and sister with food.

The most important part of this entire plan is the idea of when the human brain is most ripe for consuming. You may find this next part illogical, or even in disagreement with everything I've said thus far in this book. This is not the case however. What I am about to get into is the long-sighted vision of what it means to survive. Up until now, I've been explaining the short-sighted vision of what you need to do in order to survive as a zombie. All of that is very important. However, there is another aspect of survival, which is to remain successful and continue ever-long. The following is crucial. This is where things get interesting.

It is very important to allow humans to live until they expire of old age. You will not eat the brains of living humans, no matter what the age. I know this sounds ridiculous, but it is the future of survival we're talking about. The ideal situation, which you will manage to create through proper planning and tactical supervision, will be your working society of humans that live cooperatively within the compound that you control and maintain. These humans are your food source, but are not food until they die naturally. With enough happy humans, living within a protected society, you will find that your inventory of brains will always be plentiful.

Success will lie in your ability to manage your zombie horde. As I stated before, zombies are dumb and easily fooled, but they also have a one track mind. Their only real motivation is to eat brains. This is a difficult addiction to control in yourself as a zombie, much less each and every zombie you lead. Therefore, it is paramount that you perfect your leadership status among your current human organization. Whether you're a manager of a Wendy's or a coach of a little league team, you must have superior leadership skills and authority over this group in order to lead them, as a group, once they're zombies.

I should probably bold this entire chapter, but that would look strange, so I'll just repeat myself a bunch. Only eat freshly dead brains. Eating living brains will eventually rid the Earth of humans, and if that happens, all is lost. This is obvious if you think about it for a second, but you need to think about it for a long, long time. Once you're a zombie, you need to remember this and live the rule of eating only newly dead brains. In fact, read this chapter again. Read it over and over. I could just copy and paste this chapter over and over about 50 times, but that, again, would look strange, just like the bolding the entire chapter idea I mentioned would look strange. Just read this chapter over and over as many times as possible. If you memorize it, and you can recite it to yourself in the mirror, that's even better. Do it.

Chapter 6

Your First Moments as a Zombie 

Picture this. The Zombie Apocalypse has arrived. You have made the change and are now confused, light headed, and hungry for human brains. You look down and see that you're wearing a fanny pack. You look inside for guidance. You find gum, which reminds you of what it is to be human. You find dental floss, which is a connection to eating and maintaining hygiene. Finally, you find a whistle that you will use to summon and command your zombie followers.

Why gum? Gum is essential as it is a simple tool humans use to freshen their breath and maintain clarity in times of high stress. Some gum is even used to deliver controlled substances into the blood stream, such as nicotine and/or caffeine. The optimal type of gum you will carry in your fanny pack is up to you. Preferably you'll use gum that you enjoy as a human. Tastes and smells are connected to your sensory memory in a way that I suspect will transfer to your zombie state on some level. Your choice of gum is very important. For instance, if you remember chewing strawberry gum as a child, and your memories are pleasurable during that time, carry that gum with you. When you're a zombie and you find that gum in your fanny pack, you'll have a connection to being human and remember the ideas set up in this book, propelling your thoughts to your leadership abilities and forward towards your purpose as a zombie, which of course is your construction and maintenance of your human farm. If you hate licorice flavored gum, don't buy it for your fanny pack of supplies. As a zombie you'll most likely throw it out and forget what it was like to be human and the whole shebang is over. You'll end up as another clueless wandering zombie, eating brains where you can find them and eventually expiring, decaying on the ground. Your gum choice is very important. Choose wisely.

Why dental floss? Your hygiene as a zombie won't be that important. You don't need to brush or floss. Dental floss however will serve as another connection to humanity. Dental hygiene is something only humans engage in. Once zombies, we will have very little to connect ourselves to anything but carnivorous animals. Dental floss will function as yet another tool to bridge the gap between animal and conscience being. Most dental floss is flavored and smells minty, so that too will hold the attention of a slow, dimwitted zombie long enough to form a human memory connected to the structure of society once enjoyed. Anything that can have this type of effect on your initial zombie self to start moving on your human farm is a key ingredient of success as a zombie. The gum, coupled with the dental floss should be enough to get your arrested brain moving in the right direction.

The gum and the dental floss are tokens of society and human consciousness. These symbols serve a very important purpose while adding very little weight to your fanny pack, thus simplifying the entire experience of becoming a zombie who needs to remember humanity.

Your third artifact of humanity in your fanny pack is of course the whistle. You will use this to summon your zombie followers simply and easily. Zombies will react to your whistle. Observing you, their zombie leader, blowing the whistle, will keep them focused on you. This is all you need to keep them under your control. For instance, if a zombie has lost focus and begins to attack a human, a sharp piercing whistle blow will startle them and regain their focus on you. This will allow you enough time to hinder their advancement on the human, and then reprimand their actions however you choose. Keep in mind however, that you will also be a zombie. You're not going to be thinking clearly, or well, and you will not be quantifiably focused. When you blow your whistle, you may in fact startle yourself. Remember, as a zombie you will have a rudimentary thinking capacity, not dissimilar to a fish or domesticated bird. The ability to think is there, but we really have no understanding of how these creatures form thoughts and ideas about their surroundings, and in reality, they may just survive on pure instinct. Therefore, as a zombie with low-level understanding of what is going on, be careful with your whistle. Commit your whistle use to your deep memory. It must be a tool that will be of use to you, and not one that will confuse you.

Chapter 7

Now What?

Prepare. Discover your leadership abilities that prove successful and build upon them. Develop them. If you need help, I suggest reading Good to Great by Jim Collins. His leadership guidance is proven effective and meaningful.

Or do not heed my advice. Conclude that what you've just read is simply a humorous take on zombie culture; a simple grouping of related thoughts vomited onto these pages for reasons unknown. I certainly hope not, but if so, I appreciate the time you took to read my book.

"Without deadlines and restrictions I just tend to get preoccupied with other things." ~ Val Kilmer; Actor, Humanitarian.

Success as a zombie is similar in nature to success as a human. Many successful humans are leaders. They understand other humans and can be "The Boss". A successful zombie will need to be a "boss" as well. This won't be easy as you will read within this book, once a zombie you will become slow and dumb, or at least slower and dumber than you are right now. However, I predict you are quite intelligent if you are interested in purchasing this book. But back to what is important. Zombies don't follow each other, but rather just wonder around in packs, assumingly because none of them really know what's going on. That's where you, the successful zombie, will use your skills to achieve what other zombies cannot. This book, The Successful Zombie, will prepare you well for the impending apocalypse with brilliant methods, important artifacts, and the mindset to accept your fate. Thank you.